"Today you must take the cow to market and sell her for as much as you can," said Jack's mother.

Jack came back and told his mother that he had sold the
cow to an old woman for a bag of beans. His mother was so
angry that she threw the beans out of the window.

When Jack awoke in the morning, he was amazed to see a huge beanstalk growing outside his window, just where his mother had thrown the magic beans.

The beanstalk was so high, it reached into the clouds. Jack wondered what was at the top and started to climb up.

He paid no heed when his mother begged him to come down.

When Jack reached the top he found himself in a wonderful country. The fairies led him to the door of a huge castle where the wicked giant lived.

Jack knocked bravely on the door and told the giant's wife
that he was hungry.

The kind-hearted woman took him in, and gave him food.
Just as Jack finished his meal, the castle began to quake
and shudder.

"You must hide!" said the giant's wife and pushed Jack into a crock. Just then in came the giant.

At once he called for his pet hen. Jack peeped out of the crock and was amazed to see that the hen laid golden eggs.

By and by the giant fell asleep and Jack crept out of the crock. He picked up the hen and ran off home to his mother with it.

Next day Jack went back to the castle and saw the giant busily counting his money.

Again the giant fell asleep, and Jack picked up the bags of gold, and ran off home to his mother with them.

On the third day, Jack visited the castle once more, and the giant was playing on his golden harp. Soon he fell asleep.

Jack tried to run off with the harp, but it was a magic harp,
and cried out "Master! Master!" This woke the giant and he
ran angrily after Jack.

Jack scrambled down the beanstalk and called to his mother to bring him an axe. Then he quickly cut down the beanstalk.

The wicked giant crashed to the ground. Jack had killed the giant! And now that they had his treasure, Jack and his mother lived happily ever after.

NURSERY NONSENSE

"Hi diddle-diddle" played the Cat on his Fiddle
While the Cow jumped over the Moon
And the Dish set off for Nursery Land
With his dear little friend — the Spoon.

That night they saw the strangest sight
While the Moon was a-sailing by
'Twas the Old Woman-Tossed-in-a-Basket
Sweeping cobwebs from the sky!

Such a funny little fellow — now who can he be,
With his nightgown — and two bare feet!
"Why Wee Willie Winkie of course," said the Spoon,
"Just look — how he runs down the street!"

High in the leafy tree-tops,
When the night was bright as day,
They watched the fun and laughter
Of boys and girls at play.

Then they met the Man-in-the-Moon who said,
"Can you tell me the way to Norwich?
I must be there by breakfast time
For my plate of cold pease-porridge!"

They watched the children go to bed
While one little star twinkled bright,
As if to say, in his friendly way,
"Good-night, my dears, Good-night!"

They knelt with a dear little maid, by her bed,
And this is the prayer they softly said,
"Dear Matthew, Mark, dear Luke and John,
Please bless the beds we lie upon!"

"Shame on you, Goosey-Gander,
We've caught you unawares,
How could you throw that poor old man
And bump him down those stairs?"

Down in the kitchen they saw a sight
They'd never seen before —
'Twas the Farmer's Wife and Three Blind Mice
Who'd chased her off the floor!

Said the Dish to the Spoon in the pantry,
"I'm sure I heard a thief!
Look out — it's naughty Taffy
Trying hard to steal the beef!"

Up in the sky — a shoe sailed by,
Said the Spoon — "Now isn't that odd!"
But the Dish replied — "Why not at all
That's Winken, Blinken and Nod!"